The Poky Little Puppy's Naughty Day

Story and pictures
by Jean Chandler

A GOLDEN BOOK • NEW YORK
Western Publishing Company, Inc., Racine, Wisconsin

 Library of Congress Catalog Card Number: 82-82286 ISBN 0-307-03037-7/ISBN 0-307-60243-5 (lib. bdg.)
G H I J

Four little puppies woke up early. They knew that today was going to be a special day. They were going to visit Grandmother. They ate their breakfast, and then they went out to play.

One poky little puppy woke up much later. But he woke up feeling frisky!

At breakfast he upset his cereal bowl. Then he knocked a plant off the window sill.

"What is wrong with you today?" asked Mother.
"Nothing," said the poky little puppy. "I'm just feeling frisky, and I can't help that."
"I think you had better sit on the naughty step for a while," said Mother. "Perhaps that will help you feel less frisky."

Sadly, the poky little puppy sat on the naughty step and watched his brothers and sisters play. They ran and tumbled and chased butterflies. He wished he could run and tumble with them.

Finally Mother said he could go outside and play.
"But don't get dirty," she said. "We are going to visit Grandmother soon."
"I'll be good," promised the poky little puppy.

The little puppies ran off to play tag. One, two, three, four...but where was the poky little puppy?

He was watching a shiny blue-black beetle near the fence. He tried to catch the beetle as it burrowed into the soft earth.

The poky little puppy dug as fast as he could, but the beetle was faster. The poky little puppy dug and sniffed, dug and sniffed. Before he knew it, he had dug a hole right under the fence and into the yard next door.

Mr. Fitzrandolph's freshly washed clothes were blowing on the line. A pair of long red underdrawers danced in the breeze.

The poky little puppy caught one leg and pulled. . . and pulled. *Pop! Pop!* went the clothespins.

Away went the poky little puppy, dragging those long red underdrawers through the mud.

"Come back here!" shouted Mr. Fitzrandolph. But the poky little puppy dragged those red underdrawers all the way across the yard, until they caught on a briar bush. The thorns tore holes in the cloth.

Just then Mother came outside to gather the puppies together for their visit to Grandmother. She saw what the poky little puppy had done.

"It was naughty of you to ruin our neighbor's underdrawers," she said. "And now you are all muddy, too!"

"I'm just feeling frisky," said the poky little puppy, "and I can't help that."

Mother said, "We'll walk slowly while you go back and apologize to Mr. Fitzrandolph. Don't be long!"

The poky little puppy started back. But on the way he saw a bright blue butterfly fluttering near Mrs. LaTowsky's flower bed. Up and around and back and forth went the poky little puppy, leaping, snapping, trying to catch that butterfly. What a good game!

"You naughty puppy!" Mrs. LaTowsky shouted. "You've ruined my flowers." She aimed her garden hose right at the poky little puppy. The cold water made the poky little puppy shiver all over.

Mother came to see what happened. She was angry when she saw the flower bed.

"When we come home," she said, "you will have to apologize to Mr. Fitzrandolph *and* Mrs. LaTowsky."

The poky little puppy was sorry. "But I'm feeling so frisky," he said. "I just can't help it."

Mother and the puppies went on their way. Soon they came to Grandmother's house.

The poky little puppy ran joyfully up the walk and into the house. "Hello, Grandmother!" he shouted.

Grandmother gave him a hug. Then she saw the muddy paw prints he had made on her nice clean floor.

"I'm sorry," said the poky little puppy. "I can't seem to do anything right today. I guess I'm just feeling too frisky."

"Well," said Grandmother, "perhaps if you wash your paws and help me mop the floor you will feel less frisky."

"Yes, Grandmother," said the poky little puppy in a small voice.

After lunch, Grandmother said she would read the puppies a story. "Now where did I leave my eyeglasses?" she wondered.

While Grandmother looked for her eyeglasses, the poky little puppy looked longingly at a plate of cookies on a table across the room.

He meant only to sniff a little at the cookies, but GRASH! Over went the table, with the cookies, the flowers . . . and Grandmother's eyeglasses!

All the puppies had to help clean up the mess. When the cleaning-up was done, it was time to go home. There was no time to hear a story.

"Good-by, Grandmother!" the puppies called.

On the way home, the poky little puppy trailed behind everyone else.

"I guess he isn't feeling so frisky any more," said one of his sisters.

"Thank goodness," said the other puppies.

"Thank goodness," said Mother.

That night after dinner each puppy had a piece of Grandmother's special chocolate cake. The poky little puppy didn't upset his dish or spill a single crumb on the floor.

The next morning the poky little puppy woke up early. He took the newspaper to Mr. Fitzrandolph. He helped Mrs. LaTowsky dig a new flower bed. And he promised himself that he would try not to be naughty ever again.